The Adventures of

Aloha Bear
and Maui the Whale

By
Mark A. Wagenman

One day, under the bright Hawaiian sun, Aloha Bear sat fishing off the great coral reef.

All of a sudden, he had an adventuresome idea! He would sail around the islands in search of pirate treasure at the bottom of the ocean!

"I know I could find lots!" said Aloha Bear.

"Find lots of what?" said a voice from behind him.

Aloha Bear turned around. There was his friend, Maui the Whale and her calf, Keiki.

"Lots of pirate treasure," said Aloha Bear. "I'm going to sail around the Hawaiian Islands in search of some!"

Maui the Whale frowned. "I don't think that's a good idea, Aloha Bear. Sailing on the ocean alone can be very dangerous." she said.

"Well! I know how to sail!" said Aloha Bear.

Maui the Whale blew her spout. "You should stay close to shore where it's safe," said Maui the Whale as she turned to Keiki, who was swimming beside her.

"Come on, Keiki. It's time to go. Goodbye, Aloha Bear."

Aloha Bear watched Maui the Whale swim away. After sitting and thinking for several minutes, he decided that he would go sailing for treasure anyway!

"Maui the Whale was being silly. It couldn't be that dangerous," he thought as he walked up the beach, to prepare for his trip.

As he gathered bananas and made jelly sandwiches, his friend Turtle came by to say hello.

"What are you doing?" asked Turtle.

"I am making sandwiches for my long journey. I am going to sail the Molokai Channel in search of sunken pirate treasure."

"That's not a good idea," said Turtle. "You don't know much about sailing, and that's a very big ocean!"

"Don't be silly," said Aloha Bear. "I know a lot about sailing!"

Turtle shook his head..."Sounds too dangerous to me."

Aloha Bear didn't know very much about sailing. But that wasn't about to stop him! He ignored all of the warnings from his friends.

Aloha Bear finished loading his boat while Turtle watched.

"Goodbye, Turtle!" said Aloha Bear, setting his sail. "I'll miss you. But don't worry; I'll be back with lots of Pirate Treasure! You'll see!"

Turtle sniffed. "Good luck, Aloha Bear. I'll miss you too."

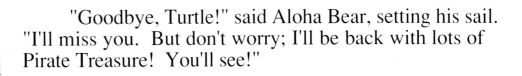

Sadly, Turtle watched as Aloha Bear's boat floated further and further...and further away.

As Turtle walked up the beach, he wondered if he would ever see his dear friend Aloha Bear again.

Meanwhile, far out at sea...Aloha Bear's little boat clung tightly to each wave as the mighty sea tossed him this way and that.

"Oh my," said Aloha Bear. "This is pretty rough for such a little boat."

But Aloha Bear sailed on, holding back his fears, trying not to think of what Maui the Whale and Turtle had warned him.

As night came, it started to rain, and the wind began to blow very hard. With each gust, it grew stronger and stronger, tipping Aloha Bears's boat from side to side.

"Oh no!" said Aloha Bear, becoming frightened, as the water poured into his boat.

Aloha Bear's boat
crashed against the waves,
moving up...

and then down,

down,

down,

as the waves grew higher and higher.
The storm became worse than anything
he had ever seen.

Aloha Bear gripped the mast of his boat
as tightly as he could, and closed his eyes.

Suddenly, a huge wave washed over his boat and dumped him into the churning water.

"Oh no!" shouted Aloha Bear, thrashing about...
"I wish I had listened to Maui the Whale and Turtle!"

Then the world began to spin!

Aloha Bear was caught in A GIANT WHIRLPOOL!

Around and around, deeper and deeper he went,
crying and shouting until finally, there was only black...

...and everthing stopped!

Aloha Bear slowly opened his eyes...It was morning. His little boat was gone. All that remained was the wooden mast, which he clung to.

The sea was calm. The storm was over, and Aloha Bear was hungry, scared and tired.

"I'm so hungry," said Aloha Bear.

"Me too," said a deep voice from behind him.

Startled by the voice, Aloha Bear quickly turned his head.

"Who said that?!" he shouted...

But nobody was there.

"Oh my," said Aloha Bear, rubbing his head. "I'm so hungry, I'm starting to imagine things."

"You're not imagining this," said the mysterious voice again.

This time when Aloha Bear turned his head, he saw two big yellow eyes staring up at him.

Surprised, he asked, "Who are you?"

"I'm your friend, and I've come to see if you'll join me for breakfast."

"Yes! I'd love to have breakfast with you! I'm sooooooo hungry," said Aloha Bear.

The voice laughed. "You don't understand. You are my breakfast!" he said, as several large tentacles rose up around Aloha Bear.

Aloha Bear grew frightened, as he looked at the giant octopus.

"Oh no, please don't eat me!" he cried.

But the giant octopus moved closer...
        and closer,
            and closer still.

Aloha Bear shut his eyes and held back a scream.

The giant octopus laughed and gripped Aloha Bear tighter.
But as he opened his mouth to swallow Aloha Bear, there was
a hugh splash of water.

Aloha Bear opened his eyes...

It was Maui the Whale!

With one giant scoop of her powerful tail, Maui the Whale chased the octopus away.

She then came to where Aloha Bear floated in the water.

"Looks like I got here just in time!" said Maui the Whale.

"Oh thank you for saving me, Maui the Whale!" said
Aloha Bear gratefully.

Keiki nuzzled Aloha Bear and blew his spout.

"I'm happy to see you, too, Keiki," said Aloha Bear.

Maui the Whale cleared her throat. "Isn't there something else you would like to say, Aloha Bear?"

Aloha Bear hung his head...

"I'm sorry for not listening to you and Turtle," said Aloha Bear. "Next time, I promise never to go sailing alone."

Maui smiled and dove into the water.

The water began to bubble around Aloha Bear. He suddenly found himself being lifted out of the water and sitting on top of Maui the Whale.

"Let's get you home," said Maui. "Turtle will be happy to see you!"

Aloha Bear smiled with glee!

And away they went! Aloha Bear sitting high on top of Maui the Whale, as she churned through the water like a mighty freighter.

Keiki followed close behind, blowing his spout, laughing and playing . . .

All happy to be going home.